# Special Times

by Sara Nephew

## Table of Contents

### Blocks

### Quilts

## Credits

Unless expressly stated, all the quilts in this book were designed, pieced and quilted by Sara Nephew.
Special thanks to the pattern testers, Joan Dawson, Jean Look-Krischano, and Shirley Lyons.

Photography....Terry Reed
Cover Graphics-Elizabeth Nephew
www.nephco.com

Clearview Triangle
8311 180th St. S.E.
Snohomish, WA 98296-4802
Tel: 360-668-4151
Fax: 360-668-6338
E-mail: ClearviewT@cs.com
http://ourworld.cs.com/ClearviewT

ISBN 1-930294-00-X

# Baby Chick

| | | | |
|---|---|---|---|
| | 1½" finished square | | |
| | 8" x 12½" block with seam allowance | | |

Cut for 1 block:

| | | | |
|---|---|---|---|
| 1. | 1 chick | 5" | square |
| 2. | 1 chick and 2 background | 3½" | square |
| 3. | 1 background | 2" x 8" | rectangle |
| 4. | 2 background and 1 chick | 2" x 3½" | rectangle |
| 5. | 9 background, 5 beak, and 2 chick | 2" | square |
| 6. | 1 beak and 1 background | 1¼" x 5" | strip |
| 7. | 2 background | 1¼" | square |

Directions:

1. Sew the 1¼" strips together lengthwise. Cut two 2" sections from this set of strips. (legs)

2. Place a background 2" square on one corner of the chick 5" square and sew a diagonal seam as shown. Outside the stitching, trim fabric to a ¼" seam. Press to the triangle. Sew a 2" background square on two more corners. (body)

3. Sew a beak 2" square on one corner of the 3½" chick square with a diagonal seam as shown. Trim and press to the triangle. Sew a 1¼" background square to each adjacent corner as shown. Trim and press to the triangle. (head)

4. Sew a chick 2" square on one corner of the 3½" background square with a diagonal seam as shown. Trim and press to the triangle.

5. Place a beak 2" square on one end of a background 2" x 3½" rectangle and sew a diagonal seam as shown. Outside the stitching, trim fabric to a ¼" seam. Press to the triangle. Make two of these. Make another from a background 2" square and a chick rectangle.

6. Sew a 2" beak square on one end of the background 2" x 8" rectangle as shown. Trim and press.

7. Place a beak and a background 2" square right sides together and sew a diagonal seam. Trim on one side to a ¼" seam allowance. Press to the dark. This is a 2" half-square.

8. Assemble according to the piecing diagram.

2

# Baby Chick

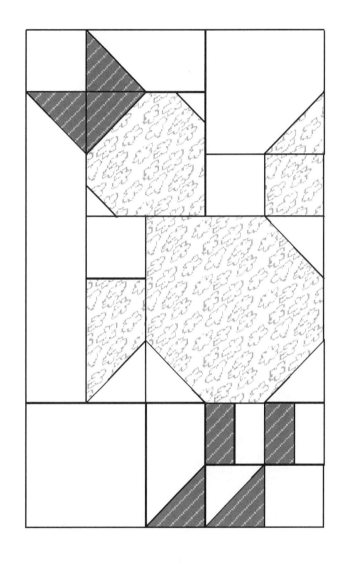

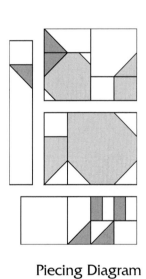

Piecing Diagram

# *Our Flag*

Cut for 1 block:

| 1. | 1 stars | 11" | square |
|---|---|---|---|
| 2. | 3 red and 3 white | 2" | strip |
| 3. | 1 red | 2" x 15½" | strip |

Directions:

1. Sew the selvage to selvage 2" strips into a set of strips, alternating red and white. From this set of strips cut a 15½" section and a 26" section.

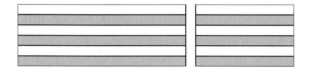

## Piecing Diagram

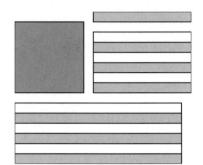

2. Assemble according to the piecing diagram.

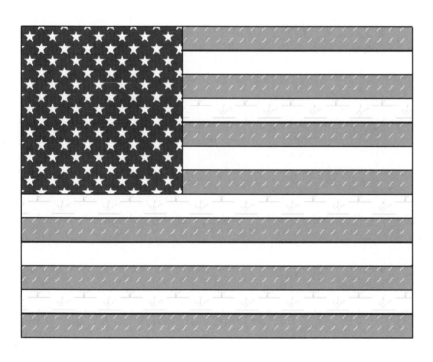

# Egg

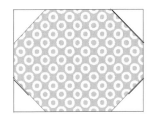

1½" finished square
5" x 6½" block with seam allowance

Cut for 1 block:

| 1. | 1 egg | 5" x 6½" | rectangle |
| 2. | 4 background | 2" | square |

Directions:

1. Place a background 2" square on one corner of the egg 5" x 6½" rectangle and sew a diagonal seam as shown. Outside the stitching, trim fabric to a ¼" seam. Press to the dark. Sew a background 2" square diagonally on all four corners to complete the Egg block.

---

# Egg Basket

1½" finished square
9½" x 11" block with seam allowance

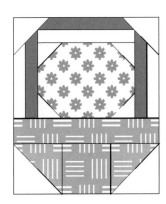

First make the egg section according to the directions above. Then cut these additional pieces for 1 block:

| 1. | 1 basket, 1 background | 3⅞" | square |
| 2. | 1 basket | 3½" | square |
| 3. | 2 background | 2¾" | square |
| 4. | 1 basket | 2" x 9½" | rectangle |
| 5. | 1 handle, 1 background | 1¼" x 19½" | strip |

Directions:

1. Sew the 1¼" strips together lengthwise. Cut three 6½" sections from this set of strips. Sew these sections on the top and two sides of the Egg block as shown in the diagram. Place a 2¾" background square at a top corner of this egg section and sew a diagonal seam as shown. Outside the stitching, trim to a ¼" seam allowance. Press to the triangle. Sew another 2¾" background square diagonally on the other top corner.

2. Place the background and basket 3⅞" squares right sides together. Draw a diagonal line on the back of the lightest fabric. Stitch ¼" away from the line on both sides. Cut on the drawn line to produce two 3½" half-squares.

3. Assemble according to the block diagram.

# Balloons

Cut for 1 block:

| | | | |
|---|---|---|---|
| 1. | 1 background | 6½" x 9½" | rectangle |
| 2. | 1 background | 5" x 8" | rectangle |
| 3. | 1 background and 6 balloon | 5" | square |
| 4. | 1 background | 3½" x 8" | rectangle |
| 5. | 1 background and 1 balloon | 3½" x 5" | rectangle |
| 6. | 1 background | 3½" | square |
| 7. | 3 background | 2" x 5" | rectangle |
| 8. | 1 background | 2" x 3½" | rectangle |
| 9. | 24 background and 3 balloon | 2" | square |

Directions:

1. Place a background 2" square on one corner of a balloon 5" square and sew a diagonal seam as shown. Outside the stitching, trim fabric to a ¼" seam. Press to the triangle. Sew a background 2" square diagonally on the other three corners. Trim and press. Make four of these. On two balloon 5" squares, sew three background 2" squares and one balloon 2" square.

Balloon Color

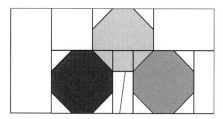

2. Sew two background 2" squares on the top two corners of the balloon 3½" x 5" rectangle with a diagonal seam as shown. Trim and press to the triangle.

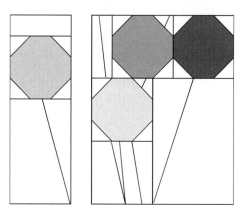

Piecing Diagram

3. Assemble according to the piecing diagram. Draw (with a Pigma ® Micron pen), appliqué, or embroider strings on the balloons according to the block diagram.

# Balloons

# Divided Cross

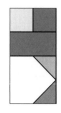

**Piecing Diagram**

Directions:

Cut for one block:

| | | | |
|---|---|---|---|
| 1. | 2 background | 6½" | square |
| 2. | 1 bud | 2" x 6½" | rectangle |
| 3. | 1 bud, 2 yellow, 3 stem, 4 flower | 3½" | square |

1. Place a 3½" leaf square on one corner of a 6½" background square. Sew a diagonal seam as shown. Outside the stitching, trim to a ¼" seam allowance. Press to the triangle. Sew a stem 3½" square diagonally on a corner adjacent to the first triangle. Make another one of these with the triangles in reverse positions. Assemble according to the piecing diagram.

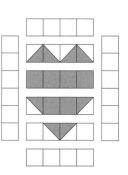

# Colorwash Heart

1½" finished square
9½" block with seam allowance

**Piecing Diagram**

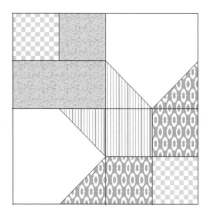

Cut for one block:

| | | | |
|---|---|---|---|
| 1. | 30 light | 2" | square |
| 2. | 14 red (dark) | 2" | square |

Directions:

1. Place a light and red (dark) 2" square right sides together. Sew a diagonal seam as shown. Outside the stitching, trim fabric to a ¼" seam. Press to the dark. Make eight of these.

2. Assemble according to the piecing diagram.

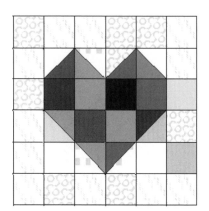

# Heart

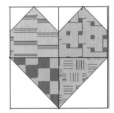

Cut for 1 block:

| | | | |
|---|---|---|---|
| 1. | 1 red and 1 background | 6⅞" | square |
| 2. | 2 red | 6½" | square |
| 3. | 4 background | 3½" | square |

Piecing Diagram

### Directions:

1. Place the background and heart 6⅞" squares right sides together. Draw a diagonal line on the back of the lightest fabric. Stitch ¼" away from the line on both sides. Cut on the drawn line to produce two 6½" half-squares.

2. Place a background 3½" square on one corner of a red 6½" square and sew a diagonal seam as shown. Outside the stitching, trim fabric to a ¼" seam. Press to the dark. Sew another 3½" background square on an adjacent corner. Make two of these.

3. Assemble according to the piecing diagram.

---

# CornerHeart

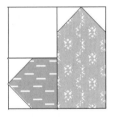

Cut for 1 block:

| | | | |
|---|---|---|---|
| 1. | 1 red | 6½" x 12½" | rectangle |
| 2. | 1 red, 1 background | 6½" | square |
| 3. | 4 background | 3½" | square |

Piecing Diagram

### Directions:

1. Place a background 3½" square on one corner of a red 6½" square and sew a diagonal seam as shown. Outside the stitching, trim fabric to a ¼" seam. Press to the dark. Sew another 3½" background square on an adjacent corner.

2. Sew two background 3½" squares diagonally on one end of the 6½" x 12½" red rectangle with diagonal seams as shown. Trim and press to the dark.

3. Assemble according to the piecing diagram.

# Angel

| | | | |
|---|---|---|---|
| | | 1½" finished square | |
| | | 14" x 18½" block with seam allowance | |

Cut for 1 block:

| 1. | 1 wing and 1 background | 6⅞" | square |
|---|---|---|---|
| 2. | 1 gown and 1 background | 5⅜" | square |
| 3. | 1 background | 5" x 6½" | rectangle |
| 4. | 2 wing and 2 background | 3⅞" | square |
| 5. | 1 background | 3½" x 8" | rectangle |
| 6. | 2 gown and 1 background | 3½" x 5" | rectangle |
| 7. | 1 halo | 2¾" x 5" | rectangle |
| 8. | 1 wing and 1 background | 2" x 6½" | rectangle |
| 9. | 1 wing and 1 background | 2" x 5" | rectangle |
| 10. | 2 wing and 1 background | 2" x 3½" | rectangle |
| 11. | 1 halo and 1 background | 2" x 2¾" | rectangle |
| 12. | 2 face, 3 gown, 1 halo, 3 wing, 5 background | 2" | square |
| 13. | 1 hair | 1¼" x 4¼" | rectangle |
| 14. | 1 halo | 1¼" x 2¾" | rectangle |
| 15. | 1 hair, 1 face and 1 background | 1¼" x 2" | rectangle |
| 16. | 1 halo and 3 background | 1¼" | square |

Directions:

1. (A) Cut the background and wing 6⅞" squares in half diagonally as shown. Sew one of each of the resulting triangles together to make a 6½" half-square. You will have triangles left for another block. Cut the background and gown 5⅜" squares in half diagonally as shown. Sew one of each of the resulting triangles together to make a 5½" half-square. You will have triangles left for another block. (B) Place the background and wing 3⅞" squares right sides together. Draw a diagonal line on the back of the lightest fabric. Stitch ¼" away from the line on both sides. Cut on the drawn lines to produce four 3½" half-squares. You will have one half-square left for another block.

(A)

(B)

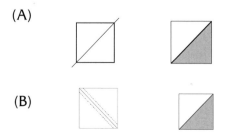

2. Sew these pieces:

A. Place a background 2" square on the bottom right corner of the gown 3½" x 5" rectangle and sew a diagonal seam as shown. Outside the stitching, trim fabric to a ¼" seam. Press to the triangle. Make one of these with fabrics reversed.

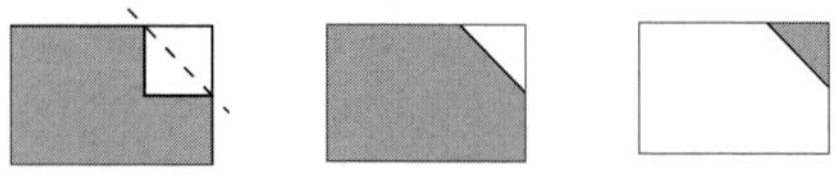

B. Sew a 2" background square on one end of the wing 2" x 6½" rectangle with a diagonal seam as shown. Trim and press to the dark.

C. Sew a wing 2" square on one end of the 2" x 5" background rectangle with a diagonal seam as shown. (cont'd on pg. 12)

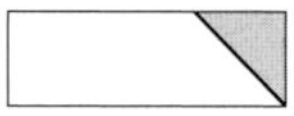

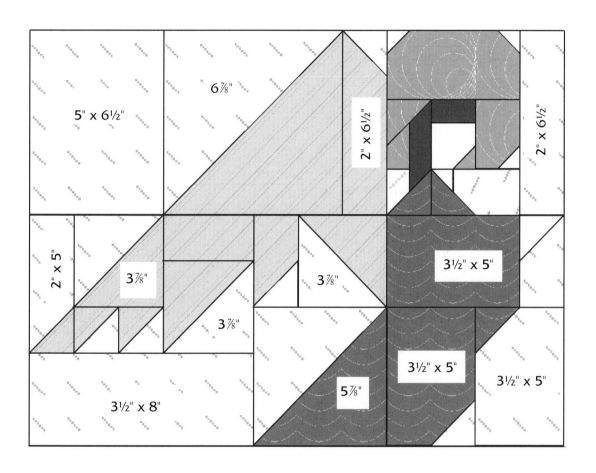

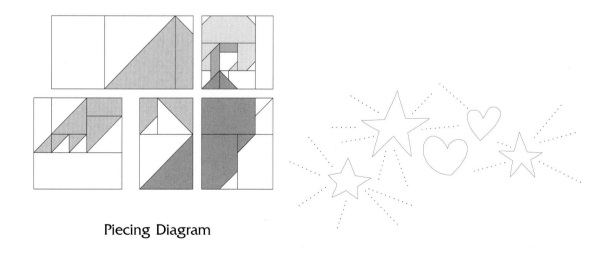

Piecing Diagram

D. Sew a face 2" square on one end of the 2" x 3½" background rectangle with a diagonal seam as shown. Make another with a wing 2" x 3½" rectangle and a background 2" square.

E. Sew two 1¼" background squares diagonally on the two top corners of the halo 2¾" x 5" rectangle as shown. Press to the halo.

F. Sew a 1¼" background square diagonally on one corner of the halo 2" x 2¾" rectangle as shown. Press to the rectangle.

G. Sew a 1¼" halo square diagonally on one corner of the face 2" square. Press to the square.

*Shoulder section:*

3. Sew the 1¼" x 2" face rectangle to the end of the 2" x 2¾" background rectangle. Place a gown 2" square over that end of the shoulder section and sew diagonally as shown. Trim outside the stitching and press to the triangle.

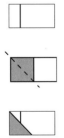

*Back section:*

4. Sew the 1¼" x 2" background rectangle onto the end of the halo 1¼" x 2¾" rectangle as shown. Sew the hair 1¼" x 4¼" rectangle to this unit lengthwise as shown. Place a halo 2" square on the hair-halo end and sew a diagonal seam as shown. Place a gown 2" square on the hair-background end and sew the same diagonal. Trim and press to the triangles.

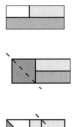

5. Place a wing and a background 2" square right sides together and sew a diagonal seam. Trim on one side to a ¼" seam allowance. Press to the dark. This is a 2" half-square. Make two of these.

6. Assemble according to the piecing diagram.

# Birthday Cake

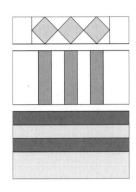

1½" finished square
14" x 17" block with seam allowance

**Piecing Diagram**

Cut for 1 block:

| | | | |
|---|---|---|---|
| 1. | 1 cake | 3½" x 14" | rectangle |
| 2. | 2 background | 3½" x 6½" | rectangle |
| 3. | 2 frosting and 1 cake | 2" x 14" | rectangle |
| 4. | 3 candle and 2 background | 2" x 6½" | rectangle |
| 5. | 2 background | 3" x 10" | strip |
| 6. | 1 flame and 1 background | 2⅝" x 10" | strip |
| 7. | 2 background | 2¾" x 3½" | rectangle |

## Directions:

1. Sew the flame 2⅝" x 10" strip and the background 3" x 10" strips together lengthwise with the flame strip in the center. Cut three 2⅝" sections from this set of strips. Offset and sew the angled sections together, lining up the three candle flames at the corners. (Pinch, check, and pin.) Cut the 2⅝" x 10" background strip in half and sew the pieces on the left and right edges of the flame section as shown. Trim into a rectangle measuring 3½" x 9½". (Be sure to leave ¼" seam allowance on all four sides. Mark center lines on the flames with chalk and line up the edges parallel to the center line.)

2. Assemble according to the piecing diagram.

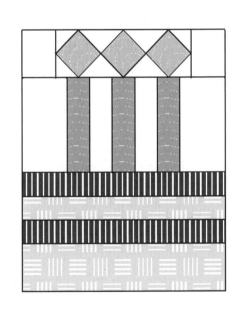

Cut 3½" sections

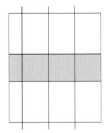

Sew, matching points

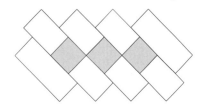

Trim to 3½" x 9½" rectangle

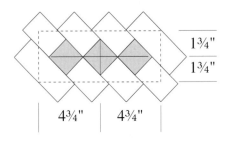

# Uncle Sam

1½" finished square
9½" x 32" block with seam allowance

Cut for 1 block:

| | | | |
|---|---|---|---|
| 1. | 1 coat and 1 background | 3 ⅞" | square |
| 2. | 1 hat and 2 background | 3½" x 5" | rectangle |
| 3. | 1 beard | 3½" | square |
| 4. | 2 background | 2¾" x 11" | rectangle |
| 5. | 1 coat | 2¾" x 9½" | rectangle |
| 6. | 1 coat | 2¾" x 5¾" | rectangle |
| 7. | 1 face | 2¾" x 3½" | rectangle |
| 8. | 1 background | 2" x 9½" | rectangle |
| 9. | 2 coat and 2 pants | 2" x 8" | rectangle |
| 10. | 2 coat | 2" x 5" | rectangle |
| 11. | 1 coat | 2" x 4¼" | rectangle |
| 12. | 2 background | 2" x 3½" | rectangle |
| 13. | 2 coat and 2 background | 2" x 2¾" | rectangle |
| 14. | 2 coat, 3 button, 4 boot, 2 face | 2" | square |
| 15. | 2 background | 1¼" x 9½" | rectangle |
| 16. | 1 hat | 1¼" x 6½" | rectangle |
| 17. | 3 button and 2 coat | 1¼" | square |

**Directions:**

1. Place the background and coat 3 ⅞" squares right sides together. Draw a diagonal line on the back of the lightest fabric. Stitch ¼" away from the line on both sides. Cut on the drawn line to produce two 3½" half-squares. (shoulders)

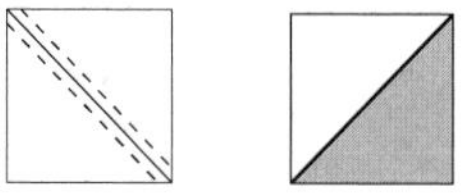

2. Place a coat 2" square on a corner of the beard 3½" square. Sew a diagonal seam as shown. Outside the stitching, trim fabric to a ¼" seam. Sew another coat 2" square at the opposite diagonal on an adjacent corner. (beard)

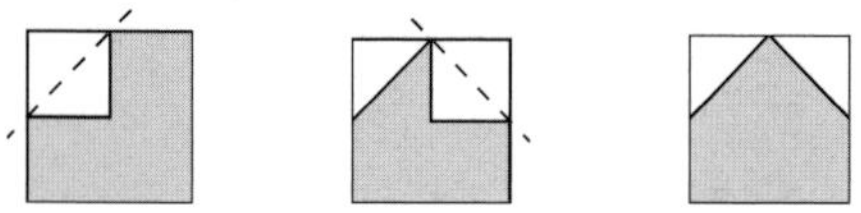

3. Sew a button 2" square on one end of the 2" x 3½" background rectangle with a diagonal seam as shown. Trim and press to the dark. Make another the reverse as shown. (coat bottom)

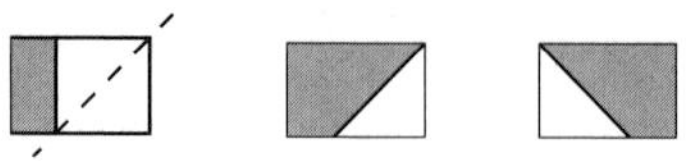

4. Sew a boot 2" square on one end of a 2¾" x 11" background rectangle with a diagonal seam as shown. Trim and press to the dark. Sew a boot 2" square on one end of a 2" x 11" background rectangle with a diagonal seam as shown. Trim and press to the dark. (toes) Assemble according to the piecing diagram.

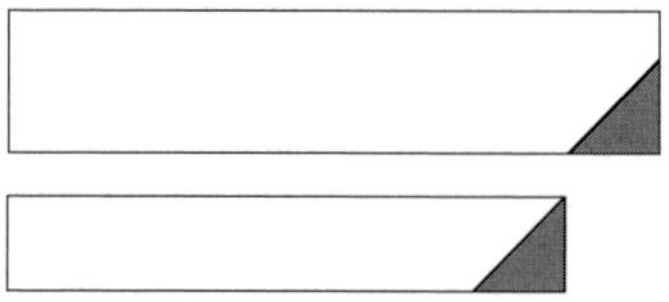

# Uncle Sam

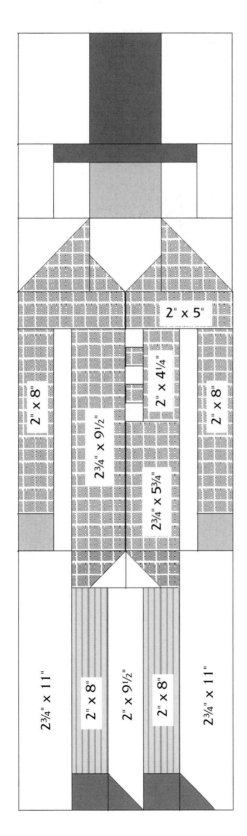

2" x 5"

2" x 8"

2¾" x 9½"

2" x 4¼"

2¾" x 5¾"

2" x 8"

2¾" x 11"

2" x 8"

2" x 9½"

2" x 8"

2¾" x 11"

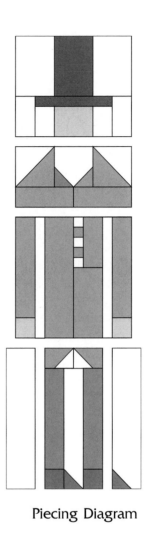

Piecing Diagram

# Sawtooth Star

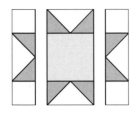

**Piecing Diagram**

| | 1" finished square |
| --- |
| 6½" block with seam allowance |

Cut for 1 block:

| 1. | 1 center square | 3½" | square |
| --- | --- | --- | --- |
| 2. | 4 background | 2½" x 3½" | rectangle |
| 3. | 8 star and 4 background | 2" | square |

Directions:

1. Place a star 2" square on one end of the background 2½" x 3½" rectangle. Sew a diagonal seam as shown. Outside the stitching, trim fabric to a ¼" seam allowance. Press to the triangle. Place another background 2½" square on the other end and sew the opposite diagonal.

2. Assemble according to the piecing diagram.

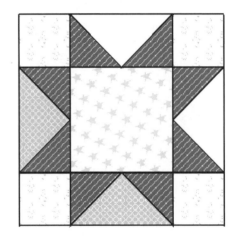

16

**Celebration**, 48½" x 56". (right) Hang this quilt for every birthday, or give it as a gift to the birthday girl or boy. Change the flavor of the cake according to your appetite. Shirley Lyons used fancy stitches from her sewing machine to make the balloon strings and also for the quilting. Let's have a party!

**Happy 4th of July**, 41" x 45½". (below) Joan Dawson chose antique-colored fabrics to add to the folk art feel of this patriotic wall hanging. Hang it for the Fourth, or hang it year-round for a country look. Try making it in red, *bright*, and blue for a more "explosive" effect. The quilting and added eyes make a face for Uncle Sam. Machine quilted by Barbara Ford.

17

**Angel Quilt**, 54½" x 62". A starry sky evokes the silence of night, and the world in peaceful sleep, while angels watch on every side. Metallic stars and busy florals put the sky together. All fabrics from Concord House. The angels are of different colors, like the wonderful differences we see in the people around us. Machine quilted by Barbara Ford.

**Colorwash Hearts**, 47½" x 57½". (top)
A friend's illness inspired the author to design this multi-patched heart block. You can make just one block and contribute it to a group quilt, or make the whole quilt – even for yourself. The many fabrics and colors included will brighten your life, and so will the sentiment expressed. Machine quilted by Barbara Ford.

**Be My Valentine**, 64½" x 64½". (right) The hearts in this quilt are actually a wide pieced border, while the floral design in the center is formed from four 12" blocks chosen from a block collection. Substitute any other 12" blocks, pieced or appliqué, for a different center design. Pieced by Joan Dawson and machine quilted by DeNae Creighton.

19

**Guardian Angel Wall Hanging**, 32" x 47½". (top left) Jean was inspired to create pink and blue angel gowns like those seen in some Renaissance paintings. With the dark borders and the warm yellow of the background, it's as if we are looking into a room filled with angels. Pieced and machine quilted by Jean Look-Krischano.

**Baby Chicks**, 44" x 42½". (top right) Little chicks peeping and brightly colored eggs in baskets are forever symbols of Spring and of Easter. Shirley chose bright pastels and an off-white background to keep the quilt light and bright. Pieced and machine quilted by Shirley Lyons.

**Easter Baskets**, 54½" x 66½". (left) The author looked for Easter colors and found stripes and silver-embellished colorful prints for the eggs. A couple of light brown directional prints made the basket weaves. You can put color in the setting strips to balance and enliven the design. Machine quilted by Barbara Ford.

# Baby Chicks

1½" finished square
Quilt with borders: 44" x 42½"

Directions:
1. Piece blocks according to the directions on pages given:
2 Baby Chick pg. 2
2 Egg Basket pg. 5
4 Egg pg. 5

2. Cut:

| 4 | 2" x 6½" | setting strip |
|---|---|---|
| 2 | 2" x 9½" | setting strip |
| 4 | 3½" x 12½" | setting strip |
| 1 | 3½" x 29" | setting strip |

All fabric 42" wide prewashed.
**Fabric requirements:**
¼ yd. chick fabric
½ yd. background fabric
¼ yd. egg fabric (or use six 5" x 6½" pieces)
⅛ yd. basket fabric
2" strip beak fabric
1¼" strip handle fabric
¼ yd. fabric for setting strips
½ yd. inner border fabric
¾ yd. outer border fabric

3. Sew the eggs and short setting strips into two Egg blocks as shown in the quilt diagram. Then sew all the blocks and medium sized setting strips into two horizontal rows. Sew the rows and the long setting strip together as shown. Add a 3½" inner border and a final 5" border to complete the quilt.

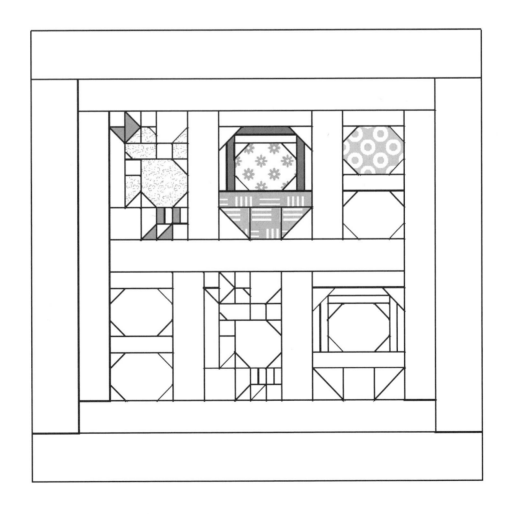

# Easter Baskets

> 1½" finished square
> Quilt with borders: 54" x 66"

All fabric 42" wide prewashed.

**Fabric requirements:**
⅔ yd. egg fabric (or twenty-four 5" x 6½" pieces)
¼ yd. basket fabric
1 yd. background fabric
1 yd. setting strip fabric
⅔ yd. inner border fabric
1 yd. outer border fabric

**Directions:**
1. Piece blocks according to the directions on pg. 5:

16 Egg                    8 Egg Basket

2. Cut:

| 8 | 2" x 6½" | background fabric or setting strip |
|---|---|---|
| 12 | 3½" x 11" | vertical setting strip |
| 3 | 3½" x 39½" | long horizontal setting strip |

3. Sew the 2" setting strips between pairs of Egg blocks to make eight double Egg blocks. Alternate blocks and vertical setting strips to make four rows. Sew the rows and horizontal setting strips together as shown in the quilt diagram.

Add a 2½" inner border and a 5¾" final border to complete the quilt.

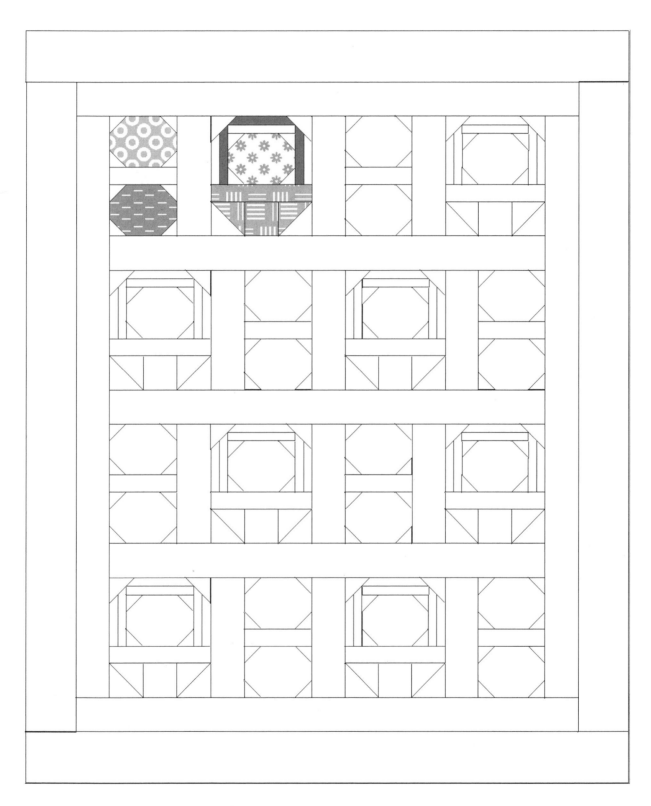

# Be My Valentine

*Any four 12½" blocks can be used for the center of this wall hanging. Try different blocks to see what kind of design they will make. The author chose a block with a floral appearance for this quilt.*

3" finished square
Quilt with borders: 64½" x 64½"

All fabric 42" wide prewashed.
**Fabric requirements:**
**For the four center blocks:**
3½" strip yellow fabric
3½" strip petal fabric
3½" strip stem fabric
3½" strip flower fabric
¼ yd. center background fabric
**For the Valentine border:**
3½" strip accent fabric
1 yd. red fabric
1½ yd. background fabric
1¾ yd. border fabric

Directions:
1. Piece four of each block according to the directions on pages given:
Divided Cross pg. 8
Heart and Corner Heart  pg. 9.

2. Cut:

| 8 | background | 6½" x 9½" | rectangles |
|---|---|---|---|
| 1 | accent and background | 3½" x 30" | strip |

Sew the 3½" strips together lengthwise. Cut eight 3½" sections from this set of strips. Sew an accent section onto the background 6½" x 9½" rectangle as shown. Make four of these. Make four reverse.

3. Assemble all the sections according to the quilt diagram. Joan added a 1½"inner border and a final 8" outer border to complete the quilt.

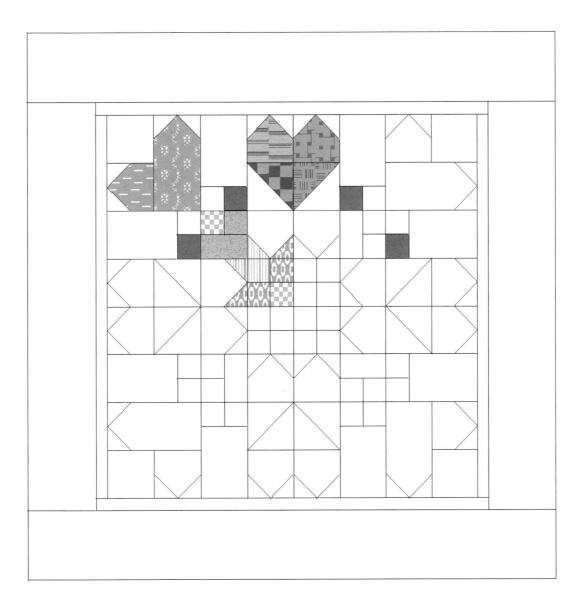

# Happy 4th of July

> 1½" finished square
> Quilt with borders: 41" x 45½"

All fabric 42" wide prewashed.

**Fabric requirements:**

scraps for hat, buttons, beard,
face, shoes, and other small details
2" strip pant fabric
⅛ yd. coat fabric
11" square flag blue fabric
¼ yd. each red and white fabric
⅛ yd. background fabric
⅛ yd. star center fabric
¼ yd. star point fabric
¼ yd. star background fabric
½ yd. setting strip fabric
½ yd. border fabric

Directions:

1. Piece one Uncle Sam block, pg. 14; one Flag pg. 6; and eight Sawtooth Star blocks, pg. 16.

2. Cut from setting strip fabric:

| 1 | 2" x 12½" | right of stars |
| 3 | 2" x 32" | right, left of man and flag |

Sew the star blocks into two rows of four stars each and sew the rows together. Add the small setting strip on the right end of the stars. Sew the flag above the stars. Sew a large setting strip on either side of Uncle Sam and on the right side of the flag-star section. Sew the two sections together. Add a 2" strip at the top and bottom. Then add a final 3½" border to complete the wall hanging.

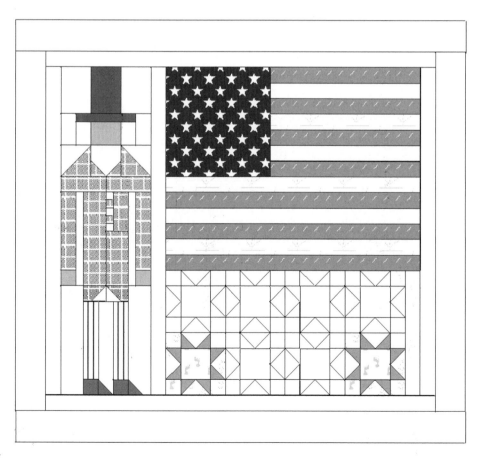

# Colorwash Hearts

Directions:

1. Piece 20 Colorwash Heart blocks according to the directions on page 8.

2. Sew the blocks into five horizontal rows of four blocks each. Sew the rows together as shown. Add a final 6" border to complete the quilt.

> 1½" finished square
> Quilt with borders: 47½" x 57½"

All fabric 42" wide prewashed.

**Fabric requirements:**
600 light 2" squares (fifteen ⅛ yd. pieces)
280 dark (red) 2" squares (seven ⅛ yd. pieces)
¾ yd. border fabric

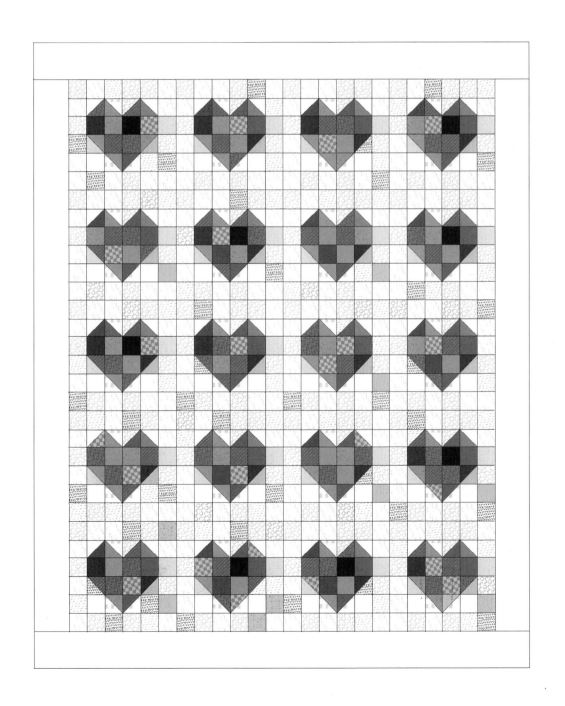

# Angel Quilt

1½" finished square
Quilt with borders: 54½" x 62"

**Directions:**

1. Piece six Angel blocks according to the directions on pg. 10.

2. Cut:

| 12 | 3½" | corner squares |
|----|-----|----------------|
| 9 | 3½" x 14" | setting strips |
| 8 | 3½" x 18½" | setting strips |

Sew the angels and 3½" x 14" setting strips into three horizontal rows as shown in the quilt diagram. Sew two 3½" x 18½" setting strips and three 3½" corner squares into a setting row. Make three more of these. Add a final 5" outer border to complete the quilt.

All fabric 42" wide prewashed.

**Fabric requirements:**

1¼  yd. background fabric
¼ yd. each three different gown fabrics
¼ yd. each three different wing fabrics
2¾" strip three different halo fabrics
2" strip each face fabric
1¼" strip each hair fabric
1 yd. setting strip fabric
1 yd. outer border fabric

# Guardian Angels Wall Hanging

1½" finished square
Quilt with borders: 32" x 47½"

All fabric 42" wide prewashed.

**Fabric requirements:**

¼ yd. each two gown fabrics
¾ yd. background fabric
2" strip of face fabric
3" strip of halo fabric
1¼" strip of hair fabric
⅓ yd. wing fabric
¼ yd. inner border fabric
¾ yd. outer border fabric

**Directions:**

Piece two Angel blocks according to the directions on pg. 10. Float each angel by sewing on a 2" border of background fabric. Sew a 2½" x 18½" strip of inner border fabric between the angels as shown. Add a 2" inner border and a 5" outer border to complete the wall hanging.

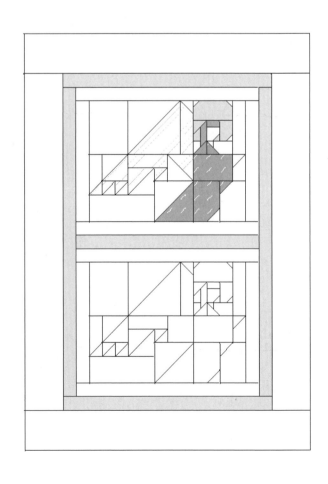

# Angel Quilt

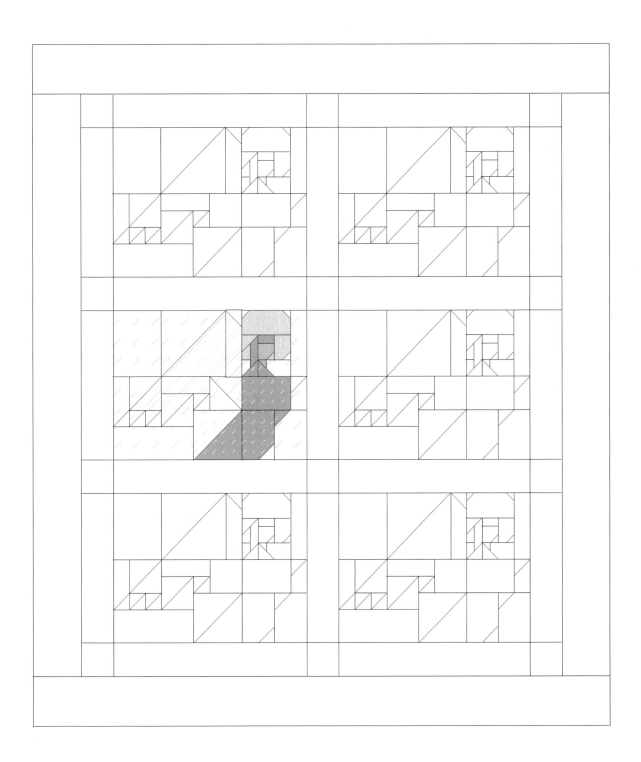

# *Celebration*

---

1½" finished square
Quilt with borders: 48½" x 56"

---

All fabric 42" wide prewashed.

**Fabric requirements:**

12 balloon fabric 5" squares plus ⅛ yd.

¼ yd. cake fabric

⅛ yd. chocolate fabric

2" strip of candle fabric

3½" strip of flame fabric

1½ yd. background fabric

⅓ yd. setting strip fabric

⅓ yd. inner border fabric

1 yd. border fabric

⅓ yd. fabric for corner squares

Directions:

1. Piece two of each of the blocks listed below:

Cake pg. 13          Balloons pg. 6

2. Cut:

| 2 | 3½" x 15½" | setting strip |
|---|------------|----------------|
| 2 | 2" x 17" | background strip |
| 4 | 5" | corner squares |

Sew the background strips to the left of one cake block and to the right of the other. Sew two vertical rows with a cake block, a balloon block, and a setting strip in each, as shown in the quilt diagram. Sew the rows together with a 3½" setting strip between. Add a 3½" inner border and a final 5" outer border, using the four corner squares, to complete the quilt.

30

# Celebration

# *Cutting and Piecing*

## General Directions

### *Tools*

You may already have most of the tools needed to piece the quilts in this book. But they will be listed and discussed one by one below so that everything necessary is ready when you begin to make your blocks.

The rotary cutter is what makes these patterns quick. Choose the brand and size that is comfortable for you to use and learn how to assemble and clean it. The author prefers a middle-sized Olfa® cutter. After using your rotary cutter carefully for a while, you will no longer dull the blade with little nicks from running over pins, etc.

Rotary Cutter

You will need a cutting mat that will keep the rotary blade sharp and protect the table or counter top. Mats come in various colors, with or without rulings on both sides. Choose a color that is easy for you to look at. Rulings are great, but at first you may wish to check the measurements of cut pieces, as the rulings on mats are sometimes not accurate.

Mats come in many sizes, too. One of the larger sizes is good for protecting a table at home, but a smaller size works better for carrying to class. (Don't leave a cutting mat in a car on a warm day.) Eventually a well-used mat will need to be replaced. But first try turning it over and wearing out the back of the mat also.

Be sure to cut at a table or counter that's the right height for you!

There are many rulers that work with rotary cutters. Three favorites are the 6" x 12", the 6" square (#6A), and the 9½" square by Omnigrid®.

The 6" square is a nice size to work with.

After all the pieces are cut, you will need a sewing machine that takes a nice straight stitch, perhaps a press cloth, and an iron and ironing board.

## *Easy Cutting and Piecing*

### Strips, Squares, and Rectangles

Cut a strip first, then cut the strip into all the shapes you need. Begin by pressing prewashed fabric selvage to selvage. Then bring the fold to the selvages and press again. Use a 6" x 12" ruler to cut a strip the desired width. The short cut needed (12" rather than 24") helps keep the ruler and the rotary cutter under your control.

Trim edge straight, then cut the strip.

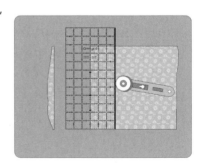

Use the top ruler edge, bottom ruler edge, or a measuring line across the ruler or on the cutting board to keep the fabric straight. Use the same ruler or perhaps a smaller square ruler to cut off the squares or rectangles needed.

TIP: If you do get a strip that's a little zig-zag, you can still cut some pieces from it (but not at the places where the strip is not straight).

## Get the Most From Your Fabric

First you will usually cut a strip to match the narrowest measure of the biggest piece. Then look for other needed pieces of the same fabric that share this strip width and cut them next.

Example: The largest piece needed is a 6½" square. So you cut a 6½" strip and cut the squares. Further down the list you see a piece needed from the same fabric that measures 2½" x 6½". So you can cut 2½" wide pieces from the same width.

Then trim the strip to the next width needed, and cut as many pieces from that width as possible. Often you'll be able to get all the pieces needed out of the first strip you cut.

Tip: Also look for pieces where two will fit into the width. Say you had a strip width of 4½", and needed some pieces 2" x 6½". You could cut a piece 4½" x 6½", trim to 4", and get two of the smaller pieces from it. Generally cut all the largest pieces first, before trimming any width from the strip.

## Shape Recognition

You will gradually begin to recognize the various sizes and shapes that you are cutting, and be able to pick them up as needed. But don't hesitate to check measurements with a ruler before sewing one piece on to another.

TIP: To prevent confusion when cutting pieces for a complex pattern, stack all pieces of the same size and pin them together. Write the size on a Post-It® note and stick it on top.

## Square On Square™ Piecing

As always, use a ¼" seam for piecing. No small triangles are used when piecing these blocks. Instead, squares are used, and sewn diagonally onto square corners of other squares or rectangles.

For example, the body of the Baby Chick (pg. 2) begins as a large square. A square of background fabric is placed on one corner of the square, right sides together and lined up accurately. Then a seam is sewn diagonally across the square, sewing it to the larger piece. The fabrics outside the stitching line are trimmed to a ¼" seam and the corner pressed out.

Making a Baby Chick Body

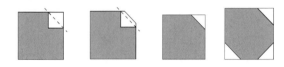

Sewing and trimming three corners results in a pleasingly rounded baby chick body. These pieces are much easier to cut and to handle than little triangles and angled pieces.

## The Most Important Seam

Square On Square™ piecing often requires the quilter to sew a diagonal seam across a small square. You can learn to eyeball the correct seam line, or try one of the tips below:

TIP: Draw a diagonal line on the back of the fabric square with pencil, chalk, or a wash-out marker.

TIP: Fold and crease the square from corner to corner to make a sewing line.

TIP: Use a ruler to draw a line with a permanent fine-tip marker (some colors do wear off after a while) on your sewing machine in front of the needle. The line should be perpendicular to the straight front edge of the sewing machine.

## Large Half-Squares

A half-square is a square divided in half diagonally (two triangles sewn together). Usually one half is dark and the other half is light. Big triangles are relatively simple to work with. They are obtained by cutting a square the size given and then cutting the square in half diagonally using a ruler and rotary cutter.

This triangle is then sewn to a triangle of another color, to get a large half-square. This requires sewing two bias edges together. Remember to handle your fabric lightly as you are sewing the triangles together. Many sewing machines sew well straight ahead. Simply laying the two triangles right sides together and gently bringing them under the presser foot with the minimum guidance required allows the machine to do the work.

Practice makes it easier. Even if the seam gets a little stretched in sewing, pressing with a steam iron or wet press cloth generally will correct any distortion.

## Small Half-Squares

In this book, small half-squares are produced by placing two small squares right sides together and sewing diagonally. The fabrics then are trimmed to a ¼" seam on one side of the stitching. The seam is pressed to the dark. If you need a lot of small half-squares made from the same fabrics, use one of the fast methods for which there are papers or templates.

TIP: If you need two large half-squares in the same fabrics, don't cut the light and dark squares in half. Instead, lay the light and dark squares right sides together, draw a diagonal line on the back of the light fabric square with pencil or a wash-out marker, and sew a ¼" seam each side of this line. Cut along the pencil line for two pre-sewn large half-squares.

TIP: The rule is usually to press to the dark. Occasionally bulky seams make it easier to press to the light.

## Speedy Strips

Strip piecing is another way to make speed and accuracy easy. To use the Baby Chick (pg. 2) as an example, the legs are produced by sewing together 1¼" x 5" leg (beak) and background strips and cutting 2" sections from this set of strips. These pieces could be all cut out separately and sewn together, but it is much easier to sew long strips together first, press them, and then cut 2" already sewn sections from the strip set.

TIP: After sewing the long narrow strips together, press the seams to the dark, pulling across the strips as you press to make sure no fabric measurement is lost in the seams. The tip of the iron helps. Then press along the strips, pulling the strip set out straight to correct any distortion from the previous pressing.

## Chain Sewing

The author used to have a sewing machine that cut the top thread with each stitch unless there was fabric under the presser foot. So I learned to chain sew. Pieces to be sewn are fed under the needle with minimum space between, and cut apart later. This speeds up the sewing and prevents the messiness of long tails of thread draped everywhere, needing to be trimmed. Many quilters keep a piece of scrap fabric to use at the start (and end) of each chain.

## Pressing Techniques

Try a wet press cloth as an alternative to the steam iron. Many experienced quilters feel that using a steam iron distorts the fabric during pressing. Use a dry iron for most of the pressing (perhaps after each seam sewn). This avoids the weight of the iron causing sore elbows and arms during extended piecing sessions.

Then when one block or unit is complete, take a piece of old sheet (my favorite, but muslin works too), dampen it in a sink, wring it out, and lay it flat over the pieced block. (The block is right side up.) Run the hot iron lightly but completely over the damp cloth to dampen the block underneath. Then lay the wet press cloth aside, and dry and flatten the block with the hot iron. You may wish to turn the block over afterwards to check that the seams are all laying correctly. Also you can tug at the block a bit as you dry it to square it up. This is like blocking a sweater. Block your block.

# Special Thanks To These Manufacturers:

**Fairfield Processing Corp.**
Cotton Batting-Soft Touch ® by Fairfield

**Quilter's Dream Cotton ™ Batting**
**Kelsul, Inc.** - Cotton Batting

**Fasco/Fabric Sales Co., Inc.**
Fabric - Marsha McCloskey's Staples ™

**Mission Valley Fabrics**
100% Cotton Yarn-dyed Woven Fabric

**Hoffman California International Fabrics**

**P&B Textiles**

**Concord House Fabric Collections**

**Rose & Hubble Textiles**

**Omnigrid, Inc.**
Omnigrid® Rulers for Rotary Cutting
Omnimat®

## Sara Nephew

Sara Nephew graduated from Alverno College in Milwaukee, WI, with an art major. She was trained as a jeweler, and showed her cloisonne' enamel work in national shows. She began her first quilt in 1967, using corduroy squares from her daughter's rompers. In the 80's she began to apply her art training seriously to quilting and in 1984 started a business making and repairing quilts.

She has since originated a series of tools for rotary cutting isometric shapes, authored 14 books, and become an internationally known teacher and lecturer. Sara now lives in Clearview, WA, with her husband, Dale. She is enjoying her three grown children and her two granddaughters. Dale is retired, and he helps in the quilting business. The couple have taken up birdwatching as another interest.

# Other Products from Clearview Triangle

## New Series - Quick Picture Quilts

| | | | |
|---|---|---|---|
| ZO 18 | $24.95 | Book - Patchwork Zoo | plus $3.00 s/h |
| HH-17 | 9.95 | Book - Happy Halloween | plus 2.00 s/h |
| TX-23 | 9.95 | Book - Special Times | plus 2.00 s/h |
| PR-22 | 6.00 | Pattern-Pigma® Pen Roll-Up | plus 1.00 s/h |

## 60° Triangle Books and Tools

| | | | |
|---|---|---|---|
| B-21 | 14.95 | Book - Sensational 6-Pointed Star Quilts | plus 2.00 s/h |
| B-10 | 14.95 | Book - Building Block Quilts | plus 2.00 s/h |
| SR-20 | 16.95 | Super 60 (Combination Triangle Tool) | plus 3.00 s/h |
| MP-3 | 11.50 | 8" Mini-Pro | plus 2.00 s/h |
| M-15 | 11.50 | Metric Triangle | plus 2.00 s/h |
| CT-1 | 8.00 | 6" triangle | plus 2.00 s/h |
| CT-2 | 13.00 | 12" triangle | plus 3.00 s/h |
| GP-12 | 5.95 | 2-sided Graph Paper-Pad of 30 sheets | plus 2.00 s/h |

## Bargain Corner

| | | | |
|---|---|---|---|
| SF – 8 | 5.00 | Book - Stars and Flowers | plus 2.00 s/h |
| EA –7 | 5.00 | Book - Easy & Elegant Quilts | plus 2.00 s/h |
| MA-14 | 5.00 | Book - Mock Appliqué | plus 2.00 s/h |
| MC-16 | 4.00 | Book - Merry Christmas | plus 2.00 s/h |
| NL-19 | 3.00 | Book - New Labels | plus 2.00 s/h |

For each additional item ordered
subtract $1 from the shipping charges.
Wash. residents add 7.6% sales tax
We take Visa and Mastercard.
Tools usually shipped UPS
Books U.S. Mail

CLEARVIEW TRIANGLE
8311 - 180th St S. E.
Snohomish, WA 98296-4802 USA
Tel: 1-360-668-4151
Fax: 1-360-668-6338
Orders: 1-888-901-4151

E-mail: ClearviewT@cs.com
Website: http://ourworld.cs.com/ClearviewT